BE WHERE FEET ARE!

To Ridge. Love, Yuppie.

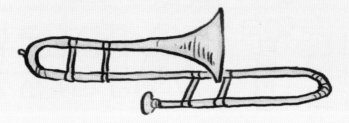

NATIONAL CENTER for
YOUTH ISSUES

P.O. Box 22185
Chattanooga, TN 37422-2185
423.899.5714 • 866.318.6294
fax: 423.899.4547 • www.ncyi.org

ISBN: 978-1-937870-50-8 $9.95
Library of Congress Control Number: 2018948315
© 2018 National Center for Youth Issues, Chattanooga, TN
All rights reserved.
Written by: Julia Cook
Illustrations by: Jon Davis
Design by: Phillip W. Rodgers
Contributing Editor: Jennifer Deshler
Published by National Center for Youth Issues • Softcover
Printed at Starkey Printing, Chattanooga, Tennessee, U.S.A., September 2018

These are my feet
and this is me.
Sometimes I'm not
where I'm supposed to be.

My brain gets crowded.
There's so much going on.
I do three things at once,
and get two of them wrong!

"Be where your feet are,"
I hear people say.
"Do one thing at a time.
It's a much better way."

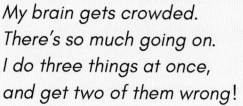

Every day, my feet get ready
for school, but the rest of me
has other things to do.

PERMISSION

HOME
WORK

4

"Is your homework in your backpack?
Did you brush your teeth?
Don't forget your permission slip
for the field trip next week."

"Remember you have a game tonight,
so hurry home right after school.
Good luck on your trombone tryout!
And try hard to follow the rules."

TROMBONE

SCHOOL RULES

My feet walked me to school, and on the way, I practiced my trombone solo in my head.

"I'm a trombone rock star!
See how I can blow!!!"
I marched right past the school,
and didn't even know!

"Hand in your permission slips,"
I heard my teacher say.
"Please place your homework in the basket,
and put your other stuff away."

I reached into my backpack, but it was empty!

"I know my homework's in here,
and my permission slip is, too.
I thought I put them in last night.
Now what am I supposed to do?"

"It's time now for our math tests,
so take out all your stuff."

Math TEST?! What math test?
Today is gonna be rough!!

My math test took like FOREVER!!!
I couldn't wait to get it done.
All I could think about was my trombone tryout.
I just wanted to be number one!

TROMBONE ROCKS!!

1) 4(382) =

2) 1475 × 27 =

3) 789 ÷ 13 =

I ran down the hall as fast as I could.
I needed all the warm-up time I could get.
I decided to cut through the gym,
and ran right into the volleyball net!

"Hey! Be where your feet are!"

I started warming up...
and then a part of me left my feet.
The next thing I knew, inside my head,
I was marching in the street.

"I'm a trombone rock star!
See how I can blow!"
All the other kids looked really confused,
and then my band teacher said...

"NO!

**Those aren't the right notes!
Be where your feet are!"**

I played my solo a few minutes later,
and as soon as I got done,
I could tell by the look on my band teacher's face.
I knew I was Number One!!!!!

WOO HOOO!!!

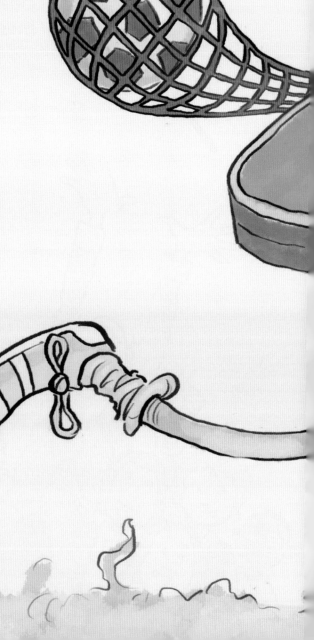

The rest of my day was such a blur.
I don't even remember walking home.
It's a good thing my feet know where I live,
because my brain was in a zone.

OOOPS! I wonder how deep this mud puddle is.

I want a bike like that.

I'll do a selfie by this cool car.

I wish I had a cat.

Just as I got home my mom pulled into the driveway.

"You're not ready? What are you doing?
Your game starts in half an hour!!
Why are you holding that cat?
It looks like you need a shower!"

"Oh, and how did your trombone tryout go?"

My soccer game was
kind of a disaster...

And after dinner, my life got even worse!

*"I just got an email from your teacher...
she said today you had a test?
You and I need to have a talk.
There's no way you did your best!"*

"I did do my best. Remember, I told you, I got the solo!"

"I'm not talking about your trombone tryout...I'm talking about your math test."

"Oh, I did my best on that, too."

"I'm sure you did with the part of your brain
that stayed attached to your feet.
But I bet you thought about other things too,
which caused your brain to compete."

"Well...I was kinda
worried about my tryout."

"During your soccer game today, what were you thinking about when that ball hit you in the face?"

"Oh, getting a cat."

"And what were you thinking about when you accidentally kicked a goal for the other team?"

"My trombone future."

"What do you think you should have been thinking about during your soccer game?"

"My soccer game, I guess."

"It's all about being present,
in everything you do.
If you can be where your feet are,
you'll be a much better you."

"When you tried out for your solo today, what were you thinking about?"

"Playing my song."

"What else?"

"That's it...just playing my song!"

"And how did you do?"

"Awesomely Amazing!"

"That's what it feels like to be where your feet are."

"When you share your attention
between two things, or three, or four,
your brain has to switch from one to the other.
And your focus is less, not more."

"And when someone wants to talk to you,
but you're paying more attention to your screen,
you're saying, "Hey, you're not worth my time."
And that's not just rude, it's mean!"

"You need to be mindful of Now,
and really take it all in.
Your feet are standing in the present,
not where you have or have not yet been."

"Take a deep breath and start to enjoy
what's right in front of your nose.
The people, the experiences, and the great expectations,
that are there to help you grow."

Give yourself a mindful moment,
and make your feet and brain a team."

"Well, how do I do that?"

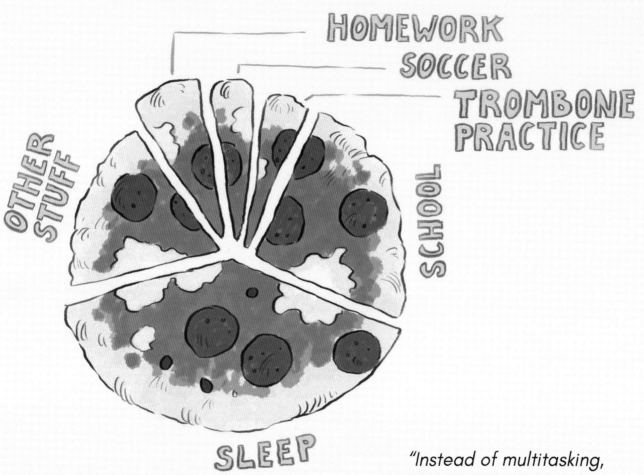

HOMEWORK
SOCCER
TROMBONE
PRACTICE

OTHER STUFF

SCHOOL

SLEEP

"Instead of multitasking,
break your time up into hunks.
20 minutes for this, 40 for that,
and some things need bigger chunks."

"Give each thing that you do ALL of your brain.
Try not to make your brain share.
Be where your feet are when you're talking to others,
and really show them you care!"

I thought a lot about what
my mom said, and decided
to give it a try.

I couldn't believe the difference,
and how much time I saved.
I got better at everything I did!
And even had more time to play!

Now I'm more mindful of what I am doing.
And it's easier to do what's expected.
I'm so much happier with myself,
because my feet and my brain are connected.

Now when someone is talking to me,
I give them all of my brain.
But my life would be so much better,
if others would do the same!

"MOM!!
BE WHERE
YOUR FEET ARE!"

Be Where Your Feet Are! – Tips for Parents and Educators

Children live in a world of distraction. Social media, extra-curricular activities, and screen time constantly compete for their attention. As a result, maintaining awareness of their thoughts, feelings, actions, and surrounding environment becomes extremely difficult. Often, we attempt trying to solve the problem by multi-tasking, but research has shown the human brain is not physiologically designed to multi-task. Doing more than one thing at a time causes the brain to switch back and forth between tasks, which actually limits productivity. Here are a few tips that can help our kids become more mindful and present in every area of their lives:

- **Be where YOUR feet are, too.** We can't expect our kids to practice and develop habits we don't model. Be mindful and appreciative of all that is going on around you and make an effort to encourage others to become more aware of NOW.

- **Never let your screen become more important than the people next to you.** In several research studies, kids have noted feeling less valued by adults because they had to compete for attention with a screen. When a child wants to talk to you...put down your phone and listen! They are important!

- **Schedule tech-free mealtimes and other activities, keeping all screens in another location.** Create memories and set a good example by talking to each other as opposed to letting the rest of the world join in.

- **Become a master at modeling, teaching, and celebrating the results of single tasking.** It may seem difficult and unproductive at first, because every time we multitask, our brain is flooded with accomplishment endorphins. But with genuine effort, you and your children will soon begin to experience the advantages of single tasking and it will become much easier to implement. Being focused and present on the task at hand is key to becoming more productive.

- **Eliminate all distractions during homework time (tv, computer games, cell phones, video games, etc.).** Allow children 10 minutes every hour to take mind breaks and check their screens in a different room, if desired, and then have them return to their work.

- **Encourage children to take a few short minutes throughout the day to close their eyes, breathe in deep, and appreciate and visualize both what they are doing now, and think through what they will transition to next.** This allows them to become more reflective, focused, and effective in the moment.

- **Avoid having devices in bedrooms overnight.** The temptation to use them unsupervised far outweighs the assumed need for sleep. Without effective sleep, a person becomes irritable, inattentive, anxious, and even depressed. Become a tech-free family between the hours of 10 pm and 6 am, where ALL family members charge their screened devices in a separate room away from all of the bedrooms.